THE GRAVEYARD SHIFT

THE DARK CORNER SERIES
BOOK 9

DAVID W. ADAMS

Copyright © 2023 David W Adams. All rights reserved.

This book is a work of fiction. Names, characters, places, and incidents are either the product of the authors imagination or are used fictitiously or in reference. Any resemblance to persons living, dead or undead, or locales are purely coincidental.

No parts of this book may be reproduced or used in any manner without written permission of the copyright owner except for the use of quotations in book reviews.

No AI was used in the writing or creation of this book.

No AI Training permitted. Without in any way limiting the author's exclusive rights under copyright, any use of this publication to 'train' generative artificial intelligence (AI) technologies to generate text is expressively prohibited. The author reserves all rights to license uses of this work for generative AI training and development of machine learning language models.

For Fran,
My truly wonderful sister, who despite everything is always there when you need her and is a true champion and unsung hero.

Content Warning

This story includes some themes or scenes that may trigger or offend those who choose to read it. Please see the list below, and proceed with caution. If any of these are triggering for you, then feel free to take breaks from the story, or turn away from it altogether. Your mental health is always the priority.

This story includes the following :

- Racism
- Blade related injuries
- Graphic depictions of injury/death
- Burial of a living person/claustrophobia
- Mutilation

While this story is of course entirely fictitious, please feel free to contact me directly through social media channels if you discover other triggering topics you think should be added to this list.

PART I

PART ONE - REGINALD

1

Have you ever seen a man's head explode under the wheel of a wagon, that has been dragged by a spooked horse running from gunfire? No? Ah just me then. I can tell you from experience, it ain't a pretty sight. There's some mighty fine things in this world. Sunsets. Sunrises. Whiskey. And of course, the company of a fine woman. But watching the top of a man's skull pop off and squirt his brains all over the dirt road like shaving cream ain't one of 'em.

But the most disturbing thing of all is, this is far from the worst thing I've seen in recent memory and I'm damn sure it won't be the worst in my future either. Somebody tried to get frisky with one of the ladies in the local establishment and had their asses handed to them by the owner. Unfortunately, it'll be poor Jimmy Ravenwood they'll be fitting for a casket tomorrow. After they scrape him up, that is.

I should probably give you a little backstory to fill

you in on the horrors of life for Reginald T. Fox. That's me by the way. Born and raised in the beautiful town of Crossroads. Of course, there was a period of time where I left this wonderful place, but more on that in a moment. Don't want you to be getting too far ahead of yourselves now, do we?

My family were involved in the construction of this place almost a century ago. Was nothing but a huge open dusty plain next to a river when they arrived. Life had been unkind to them living in the big cities, and they came across some like minded folk on the way across this vast country and together they built Crossroads. Everyone seemed to be happy here all the time, almost like there was some kind of purification of the soul once you crossed the town limits. Probably all sorts of minerals in the water and crystals in the soil, but I'm not one for all that spiritual bullshit. I believe in what I can see in my own two immaculately crafted palms of ebony brilliance. Hands like shovels they are, just like my grandpa. This place saw its fair share of violence once it became known there was a new town and no official jurisdiction. Bandits, looters, cowboys, you name it and at one time or another, they all came, but the locals stood firm. This was their home and they weren't gonna give it up.

And they didn't.

My great grandfather appealed to the nearest city for them to accept jurisdiction and we got ourselves a Sheriff and he got himself an office built. After that, we had no real problems at all. Now as for me, well old

The Graveyard Shift

Reginald T. Fox is what you would call a mild mannered man. Good with people, bad for tolerating their bullshit, but good enough to keep my cool. Got myself a job in the post office. Seen my fair share of weirdos and misguided souls come through there too. I remember on one occasion when a very attractive blonde woman and a dark haired woman, slightly younger came in one day asking to mail a letter to an address that didn't exist yet, but not to send it out for over a hundred and fifty years!

I had fun with that one. Told them that nobody anywhere was dumb enough to hold on to a letter for that long! Then I was told by my very stern boss, a Mr Johnson, that there was indeed a branch of the post office that dealt with such requests. Apparently its for those who like to make time capsules or leave advanced wills and such. He even took me to see it. The amount of letters, packages and notices filed on those shelves filled the room from floor to ceiling. Some of them were not marked to go out for almost fifty years, and while this letter in particular to someone named Silverton going to some place called Wealdstone would not leave for much longer than that, it was added to the collection. Thought about asking the blonde woman on a date, but never saw her again. Shame.

Anyway, I've waffled on long enough.

The post office is my daytime job, something to earn a little extra money. It allows me to do luxury things like eat each day, and pay my dues. My main job is a gravedigger. Hence the hands like shovels. I use one every damn day. You see we had an outbreak of some kinda virus not too long back and the existing gravediggers were older and couldn't keep up so I was taken on as an extra hand when I was just a teenager, and then the old folks died out and it was just me. My wages tripled though, so I buried those two folks with that extra bit of respect in my gratitude.

The graveyard shift is the quietest time of the day. I start at six in the evening and I head home at six in the morning. I work Monday through Saturday and take the Lord's day off. Can't have me working on a Sunday, absolutely not. I had that put into my contract. Oh yeah I got me one of them fancy signed documents. It was the Sheriff's idea when it became just me. Something to help keep the privacy of some of the folks who for example may have been married when they had a heart attack in the bed of a lady of the night. Saves all the embarrassment keeping me quiet, so I had the Sunday clause put in there for me. You scratch my back and I'll scratch yours. He was happy to oblige, and so was I. I didn't need to be up in everyone's business anyhow. Got my own shit to deal with.

Now this was the year of our lord 1886, and yet Crossroads still didn't have this new fangled electricity I'd been hearing so much about, and so I was walking around every night with an oil lamp, which ain't exactly light in weight by the way, and a huge iron shovel, and it had been a long week. A shootout in the saloon had provided me with four dead drunks to deal with, and they were all shot on a Saturday evening. This meant I

The Graveyard Shift

didn't finish my work until well into Sunday morning. I got pissed, lost my temper with the Sheriff, and I quit. Just like that. Never lost my temper like that in my life.

Well, I did once. I swore I'd never do what I did that night ever again. But I digress.

I had no idea where to go, and I had no family left. My parents had been killed not long after I was born, and I was raised by my brother, Theodore. He was a good man. But he was stupid. Found him with his throat slit in the bed of a married woman just over five years ago. Such a waste. But with nothing left to keep me in Crossroads, I hopped out of town and ended up in San Francisco.

And that is when I met Samuel Seacroft, and I ended up embroiled in murder.

2

"Have a seat, Mr Fox."

Samuel Seacroft was most definitely not an American citizen. And if he was, those papers had to have been fucking good forgeries. I don't know much about places of the world, but even I knew that Samuel Seacroft was English. I swear this guy had a literal stiff upper lip. He was a well presented gentleman, I'd say just over six feet in height, and his hair was perfectly straight and cut short to his head, with not one follicle out of place. The first time I met him, I thought this son of a bitch wouldn't last five minutes in a saloon back home. But, he did have a job opening that I was interested in, so I sat down as instructed, and listened to his pitch, all the time trying not to giggle at the over the top accent.

"Now as you know, we have many cemeteries here in San Francisco, and I for one would like you to consider joining the team of workers who look after them. Tending grounds, digging the holes and such."

"So, a gravedigger."

He looked at me as if he didn't like the simplicity of the actual job title. I didn't give a shit, it was a job I knew, and I was damn good at it. But he seemed reluctant to dumb it down for the simple folk and so tried to weasel his way out of it.

"Well, I wouldn't bring the job title down to that level, Mr Fox. There would be other duties, such as planting the borders, cleaning the headstones, general tending of the grounds, that sort of thing. Actually digging graves would be just one aspect of a many varied potential career."

Was this mother fucker for real? Who in the hell ever heard of somebody digging graves and then ending up with some kind of gold plated legacy. But I figured I could use his rambling nonsense to make this better for myself. So I spent the next thirty minutes laying out how all of that seemed like a lot of work for one man, and the money on offer really didn't match the workload. He doubled it. Then I said how I did not work on Sundays, and he was happy to have that inserted into my new agreement, and tried to tell me all of the churches I could go to for worship. I told him to go fuck himself, but in a more eloquent manner obviously. I still wanted the job. I had nothing here. He bent his ass over and gave me everything I wanted, got me to sign on the dotted line, and then said he knew somebody renting a room and would give me the address.

I should have said I'd find my own place.

I rolled up outside at five thirty in the evening, and the coach driver who took me from the administration office to the house handed me the keys with the tag attached reading *13*. I should have known right then that this was bad shit. Number 13? For a gravedigger? But I was tired, so I headed up and opened the door to the room. The smell was instant. It was like being hit full on in the face with a bag full of shit. That stench invaded my nose, throat and my eyes were stinging like somebody slammed a cactus into me. I went to back out, but ended up pushing the door shut with my ass and was stuck in there. I yanked my shirt up over my nose and mouth and slowly moved forward looking for whatever the fuck smelt like death in there.

Turned out, it was death.

3

I must have stood in that one spot for almost ten minutes. I didn't move, I didn't even realise I was still breathing until a rogue fly wandered its way into my throat and I ended up spewing my guts out all over the floor in reaction to it. Lying on the bed, which I could see through the next doorway, was a body. Or at least what used to be a body. The face looked like a man, but honestly it was difficult to tell. The level of rot which now inhabited the corpse had melted away most of the flesh and the organs on display looked like the flies had liquified them too. All of this disgusting soup had then soaked through the mattress and onto the floor where it had pooled, congealed and was now eating away at the floorboards.

That's pretty horrific right? Baby, I'm just getting started.

When I stumbled forward, I tripped on my own feet

and as I put my arm out to steady myself, I plunged down the closet doorhandle, and out flew another body. Instinctively I both tried to move out of the way but also, being a person tried to make some veined attempt to catch it. That second part was a mistake. This bag of human goop, hit me square in the jaw, and the contents of their now open skull poured directly into my mouth and down my throat. I have never squealed, scrambled and thrown up like that in my entire life neither then or since. I fell onto that floor like a pile of manure and heaved until I felt my stomach lining start to tear. The second body was still laying on my legs, and my clothes were soaked through but there was no way I was moving until every single fraction of bodily matter was out of my own body.

By the time I was done slipping in and out of consciousness, and slipping in and out of entrails, I had discovered two things.

1. There were a total of five bodies in the apartment in various stages of melting and rotting.
2. Nobody came to help me.

I banged on every single door in that building, and there were no noises, no sounds of any kind and no signs of any people. Then I noticed how every doormat had a layer of thick dust on top of it. Nobody heard me scream and nobody came to help *because there was nobody to help*.

The Graveyard Shift

By the time I composed myself enough to break open one of the other rooms, dive in their bathroom (which happily was not occupied by the body of a victim of a gunshot wound to the face) and changed into non blood-soaked clothes, it was almost nine-fifteen. My first reaction was to get the fuck out of there! But for some reason, that I cannot fathom even to this day, I felt like I couldn't leave even if I wanted to. Seacroft told me about the room to rent, and it was his driver that gave me the key. This was no mistake. Out of every empty room in this place, he gave me number 13. He did it on purpose.

My mind ran wild with thoughts of traps and being the next victim of room 13 for another half an hour, before I must have exhausted myself and passed out in the living room of room 9. But when I woke up, I nearly shit myself there and then. Samuel Seacroft was sat in the rocking chair directly opposite me, smoking a pipe and smiling.

"Good morning Reginald."

I glanced around the room, and there was nobody else, just him. I could see the top of the carriage just outside the window, and as I stretched to get a better view, I saw his driver, the one who had given me the key to room 13.

"Good fucking morning yourself, you fucking English psycho!"

I admit, my nerves and my temper were both shot. But it didn't seem to phase Samuel at all. In fact, he smiled *more*. I had no words left to say, at least not coherently, so I let him speak for a while, if only to try and figure out how I was gonna leave this place in one piece.

"I see you met our guests last night," he said so calmly, taking several puffs from his pipe, the smoke beginning to float in my direction. "Yes, awful shame about that. Then again, I had to store them somewhere. I've something of a reputation you see, and if people were to know that I'm... well... you know."

I presumed he meant killer or murderer, but the words wouldn't find their way out. Surely, he was rich enough to cover it up himself. Why would he need to keep them in a room and then send me in there, fully expecting me to freak out. What was his plan? Happily, he told me.

"You see Reginald, I have certain... desires. No perhaps desires is the wrong word. I have... interests. You see I always wanted to be a man of medicine. A surgeon actually. It was something of a fascination for me to dissect little creatures when I was a child, and see how everything ticked inside. Sadly after a while, it became more of an obsession and I quickly discovered that it wasn't the actual surgery that made me feel complete, it was the taking of the life. Whenever I cut a person's throat, or pulled the trigger so close to somebody's face that it left nothing but shattered bone behind, I felt a rush of euphoria."

I am gonna die here. This is how my life ends. Trapped in the slaughterhouse of a mad Englishman.

The Graveyard Shift

That is not what I saw being carved onto my tombstone. How did I walk into this?

"The gentlemen you saw in your room, oh and I hope you do forgive my little practical joke having them waiting in there for you, were my previous graveyard staff."

Same shit, different place. He increased my wages because I would be working on my own. Just like Crossroads. Damn how I wished I had never left at this point. Even Sheriff Daniels would be a welcome sight right now.

"You see Reginald, they discovered a few bodies here and there that weren't on their schedule, and started asking questions. Well I lost my rag, quite frankly, and whipped out this little blade here, and flash! Right across one of their throats."

He slid a long and needle tipped knife out from within his cane. The stick itself I had not noticed up to this point, but the handle was a white serpent, and served as the hilt of this miniature sword.

"Well one of the others saw me, and naturally he had to go. And by that point the bloodlust was upon me and so I dispatched the two brothers, before my groundsman knocked my cane away from me and grabbed his shotgun. Well, I may be a mere Englishman, but I soon had that weapon pointed at his own face, pulled the trigger and then bye bye face!"

The sniggering laughter made me wanna throw up again, but there was nothing left to bring up. I had to interrupt this macabre story before I passed out again or I genuinely felt I would never see the streets again.

"Why me?"

Samuel's eyebrows shot up.

"Why you dear boy? Well it had to be you! You were new in town, and so nobody knows you, and I knew if I made you aware of my nocturnal activities immediately, then you would not be able to leave. Then we would both have a secret to keep."

Apparently, there was more to throw up.

After I had taken a large gulp from the glass of water I had gotten the previous night, I wiped my mouth and tried to look directly at Samuel. It was an uncomfortable task. He knew.

"Look Samuel, I don't know what you think you know, but I-"

Like lightning, he launched his blade through the air at such a precise angle that it nicked my right shoulder enough to draw blood, but no more, and then embedded itself in the wall behind me. I could hear it wobbling left to right as it dispelled the movement.

"I know exactly what you did Reginald. How would the good folks in Crossroads feel if they knew that you, their mild mannered post office clerk and gravedigger by night was a cold blooded killer?"

There was that smile again.

But there was no escaping it. He knew. He may not know the circumstances, but he knew about my secret. My past. Something I had wanted to remain locked away forever, never to be revealed to the world. Before

The Graveyard Shift

I could speak, Samuel leapt to his feet, crossed the room and pulled his blade free before sliding it back into his cane, which locked shut with a click. He leaned in and tapped his hand on my shoulder. That spot went instantly cold, and my temples began to throb.

"Time to get yourself on task, my dear boy. Tonight, your first watch will include the burial of five bodies."

4

The fact that the coach driver was fully aware of Samuel's activities, as he described it, made me feel somewhat more trapped. This man showed no emotion at all, as he helped me lift each mangled and melted corpse into the wagon after dark. There was a rear exit where he could park out of sight, which Samuel had taken great delight in telling me that it was the same way they got them into my room for the supposed 'practical joke.'

There was no communication between us, he simply helped load them in, drove me to the edge of the cemetery grounds, and left. I had to break into the equipment shed, because the driver had not left me a key. Let me tell you something, digging five graves in one night is the work of a young man. I was no elderly miser, I was only in my early thirties, but that certainly took it out of me. Thankfully, the driver let the horse attached to the wagon so I was able to drive it up to the burial point. It was almost sunrise when I dropped the last blood soaked bundle into the final hole. This bastard wasn't even going to hide their deaths. He had bribed the local police not to investigate, and then claimed his staff were murdered by graverobbers, and he had taken care of their swift burials to help aid the families and their grief to move on quicker. Even had the gravestones all laid out by a nearby tree.

I slumped on the ground, exhausted, and watching the sun come up, thinking to myself just how I might get out of this. Yes, he knew what I had done many years earlier, and yes I had just buried five of his victims with no police consent. But would he follow me back to Crossroads if I ran? How did he know in the first place? I had only been in San Francisco two nights before meeting him, so he must have known I arrived somehow. Perhaps the person I spoke to in the bar down by the bay had mentioned to another that I was a gravedigger, and it got back to him that way. But surely not in time for him to send word to Crossroads, find out from some unknown person about me, and then send word there was a job available for me. And even then, to murder five men and move them to my room, and for them to be that far gone in such a short time? No there must be more to this than I knew of. And that is what kept me there.

I tapped the fresh dirt down on grave number five at eight a.m. exactly and headed down the hill to Samuel's office. He was sat on the porch in a chair, swaying back

The Graveyard Shift

and forth. If I didn't know better, I'd have said he'd been there all night. Watching me.

"Excellent job there Reginald, I must say. You're going to work wonders here, I'm sure of it."

"Samuel, I wanna know how you found out about me."

It is the first level of conviction I've been able to find since I left our initial meeting thinking I'd gotten everything I had demanded. Back when I felt quite proud of myself. Now of course, things were different.

"The man you murdered. He had a sister."

A flashback raced through my mind of the night in question. I had spent so many years trying to black it all out that I could only see fragments. A large hulking man leaning over a woman. A necklace. A scream. Blood. So much blood. And me holding a severed chair leg. I don't remember anyone else being there.

"A sister?" I manage, albeit weakly.

"That's correct Reginald. A sister who saw the whole thing. A sister who was married to a handsome young chap fresh off the boat from England."

I had only eaten lightly since the previous night, but it was beginning to make its way back up my gullet as those words wormed their way into my ears. Again, I tried to replay the moment in my mind. Then I saw it. The chair I had kicked to get the broken wooden leg. There had been someone sat in it at the time, and they'd rolled under the table out of sight. Presumably the sister. I looked at him with recognition.

"You were her husband?"

He nodded, and for the first time, his smile faded as he too started to recollect those events.

"She had been visiting her brother while I moved my things into her house. We had not been married long, but I adored her more than anything. She of course, did not know about my 'other' life. There was no need for her to. But when she saw you batter her brother's skull into the wood, and the blood spray up the walls coating their family pictures, it broke her. She ran out after you left, and burst into the front door telling me everything. I tried to calm her, but she didn't relax and she couldn't stay still. I woke up the next morning to a note on my pillow. All it said was 'Sorry.' I found her swinging from the beam above the kitchen table."

My gut clenched again, but I managed to keep the food down. I swallowed hard, and the noise it made caused him to look up at me.

"So I decided that I couldn't stay in that home, and left Crossroads almost as soon as I arrived. Found my way here and carried on my 'hobbies' in a much wider setting. And then I heard you had arrived. I couldn't believe my luck."

One man's luck is another man's damnation. I'd learned that during that fateful night fifteen years earlier. Now it seemed the Lord was punishing me, albeit in a rather ironic twist.

"That night," I began, "I had followed Jean to the brother's house. I'd been sweet on her since school, and she'd always hinted she liked me back. And then…"

And it was at this point, the whole grisly scenario snapped back into my mind like flicking a switch.

I remembered everything.

5

Fifteen years later

I knew I shouldn't have drank quite so much, but I was celebrating. It's not every day that your best friend gets engaged. Ralph and I had been close since we were boys. We had grown up together, gone to school together, fished in the river together, even went on dates together in our mid-teens. I was so proud of him to have finally found someone he could truly love in Eloise. They had met at a barn dance just six months ago, and yet it was obvious to everyone that they were made for each other. I had hoped to find that for myself. But that would require actually saying something to the object of my affections rather than staring at her with a goofy grin every time we saw each other. Despite all of this, I do think she knew how I felt. It was glaringly obvious. Even my brother used to tease me about it.

I patted Ralph on the back and he headed out of the saloon and off towards his house where he would be spending the night alone, as his parents were off on a mail run. It was a job he had been keen to follow in their footsteps with. See the wide open country on horseback, and he had even convinced Eloise to join him so like his parents, they were husband and wife couriers. As I walked out of the saloon myself, I saw Jean wandering down the other side of the street past the general store. I waved, but she didn't see me, and when I tried to call after her, the booze nearly made a sudden and violent reappearance, so I closed my mouth and swallowed it back down. Whiskey kind of loses it appeal when you've swallowed the same batch twice.

I slowly jogged along the street, failing to keep up or even walk in a straight line. From where I was, huddled over by the Sheriff's porch, I saw her knocking on Ralph's door. Seconds later, it opened and she went inside. I thought this was strange because to my knowledge, Ralph barely knew who Jean was. But given this was my best friend, and my future sweetheart we are talking about, I figured they were planning some surprise for me, such was my drunken stupor at the time. I staggered across the street and after a good five to ten minutes, I landed up against the wall of Ralph's house, and knocked on the door. I saw movement through the window near the dining table, but couldn't recognise who it was. I knocked again, and this time I caught the woman's attention. She was only about eighteen herself, so maybe a year or so difference between her and Ralph. I figured she was a cousin or other relative.

"Hi, can I help you?" she asked sheepishly.

"Hi, I'm Reg! I was just wondering if I could have a word with Ralph. I'm gonna be his best man, and I think I saw Jean come in here too."

The girl seemed unsure, but nodded, and let me in.

"They went in there," she said and pointed to his parents' bedroom.

"That's weird," I said, completely devoid of any thought process whatsoever. "Wonder what they're doin' in there?"

The woman shrugged her shoulders and sat down at the table, and started to knit what looked like a scarf. Winters were harsh here and you could never have too many woollen clothes or scarves. I stumbled forwards, and opened the door to the bedroom.

And the drunkenness went away, and all became clear.

Ralph was hunched over the mattress, his bare ass cheeks moving in the air, and I knew the voice moaning beneath him before I moved to get full confirmation. Ralph was fucking Jean. And she was enjoying it. I didn't move for what felt like an eternity, during which time, they both lost more of their clothes. Jean was now all but naked, her tits bouncing in his face. My own face felt red hot. Fire flowed through my veins, and I grit my teeth. It was then, that Jean noticed me standing there, and she shrieked and pushed Ralph off her, grasping for a blanket or shred of clothing to cover herself up. But the true horror came in the form of Ralph's own face. He was mortified to see me standing there. He couldn't believe that of all the people who could've caught him ploughing my schooltime sweetheart into his parent's mattress, it was me. He knew how I felt about Jean, and he still went through with it. Not to mention poor Eloise.

I stormed out but didn't get to slam the door, as Ralph caught it, pulling his shirt back over his head, his belt buckle still hanging open.

"Reg! Wait!"

I burst toward the front door, but his hand reached forward and grabbed my arm, pulling me back. I swung my fist, and it connected with his jaw, forcing him to let me go, but he came back again, and tried to hold me in place despite sporting a now split lip.

"Please, Reg, you have to stop! It was Jean!"

"What the fuck did you just say?" I growled at him.

Jean had now emerged from the bedroom in more or less her fully dressed state, red marks visible on her arms and tears streaking her face. She looked like he'd roughed her up a little, which only made me wanna kill him more.

"Reg! Stop him please!"

A noise sounded behind him, and Ralph rounded towards her, and I had never seen his face so angry as I did right in that moment. I heard a voice speaking, but my mind was so fragmented, I didn't hear what was said.

"You shut your fucking mouth. You knew what you

were doing, and you didn't care about anyone, so stop pretending!"

More tears welled in Jean's eyes as she looked at me and then back to him, and then behind her. The next part was a blur but she open hand slapped Ralph across the face with such force that he actually shifted more than he did when I clocked him in the jaw moments earlier. But that was a mistake. Ralph had never had a good temper. He brought his own fist up from his waist and swung it forward. I didn't see the impact, but I heard it. Jean was quickly on the floor. The images moved so fast I couldn't anchor myself to separate the bodies or the motions. I watched as he leapt on top of her, and grabbed hold of her necklace, pinning her throat with it.

And that's when I truly snapped.

The next few moments went by so quickly, it was as if somebody else was controlling my actions. I lunged forward and kicked by foot into the chair leg the woman was sitting on, and the chair gave way as the leg snapped free. I reached down, grabbed it, and launched myself at Ralph, swinging the chair leg above me and bringing it down with a crunch on the back of his head. One blow was enough, but I raised it and clobbered his head again and again and again. I was consumed by the betrayal, the pain, and the rage.

I didn't even stop to realise that Jean was already dead. He'd killed her just before I struck the initial blow. By the time I was done, Ralph's head no longer resembled a human's and the mess covered both Jean's body and the floor. I dropped the leg and stood back, unaware that the other woman was now watching in horror from under the table. When I realised what I'd done, I staggered backwards until I reached the door, felt for the handle, and made my way out into the night.

6

"When my wife told me about it all, I went back the next morning after the undertaker had taken away her body, but the house was empty and clean."

I nodded, a single tear now making it's way down my cheek. It had taken everything I had to go back there in the early hours and drag Ralph's body onto the cart with Jean's and drag them out to the cemetery.

"I buried Ralph under the tallest tree in the place, and I sat Jean's body down by the grave of her mother. I made it look like she had gone to visit and been attacked. Then I went back and cleaned the house. Nobody knew."

"Except his sister."

I hadn't even known Ralph had a sister. He never mentioned her, his parents never mentioned her, so where did she come from? Samuel informed me that she had been sent away when she was five years old to live with her grandparents in Plymouth in England because she was too disruptive. They thought a good old English boarding school would straighten her out. She finished school, met Samuel, fell in love and they married. She had only just landed back in America when I bludgeoned her brother to death in front of her. So I effectively killed three people that night, even if only one was directly by my hand.

Samuel stood up from his chair, dropped his pipe and walked right up until he was mere inches from my face. The stink of the tobacco smoke bore into my very skin. His right hand grabbed me by the throat, and squeezed until it became difficult to take a breath.

"You took my beloved from me. And now, you're going to spend the rest of your days cleaning up my mess and making sure everything remains nice and tidy. Keep it up, and I might even let you live."

He let go, and I felt all of the weight go out of my legs, clattering forward and landing on my knee. Samuel turned and walked into his office. I took a few moments to catch my breath, and then walked off down the path to the main street. And then, in a split second decision, I did something I shouldn't have done.

I ran.

7

Despite the threat of my violent death, the revelation of my actions and all of the proposed hellfire that came with it, I chose to return to Crossroads and face the music.

But the music never came.

I apologised to the Sheriff, who since I left had split from his wife and was no longer in a mood to bear grudges, and I picked up my old shovel and continued on with my old life. Every morning I went to bed thinking I would wake up to my bed surrounded by the law, or even worse, see Samuel Seacroft hanging over my bed with his blade just in time to slit my throat. But none of that happened.

In the couple of weeks I had been gone, nobody had replaced me and there had been six deaths in that time. Three from old age, one from a gunshot to the chest (another bar brawl in the saloon), one from a snake bite, and Jimmy Ravenwood. Turns out, they had scraped him up off the road, put him in a casket and left him in the undertaker's office for two weeks. He was mighty glad to be rid of that I can assure you. So when the night fell, and everyone had said their goodbyes, none of them having family willing to go through with a funeral, I settled in for a long graveyard shift.

By eight, I had dug two of the graves. Being back on my own turf had given me a huge sense of relief, and I seemed to work faster because of it. There was also no pressure from anyone else. It was agreed I would bury four tonight and then the most recent two tomorrow. I decided to lower Jimmy and the snake bite lady into their new homes before starting the third hole. It sounds weird, but it was getting a little chilly, and my instinct said 'don't let them get cold.' Stupid, I know, but that's the human brain for you.

As I slid the shovel into the dirt to make the first groove in the dirt for hole number three, I heard what sounded like dirt crunching beneath feet. I stopped, looked around but saw nobody. The wind was whipping up now, so I put it down to that, and thrust the shovel blade into the dirt once more. Minutes later, the wind briefly died down, and I heard the sound again. This time when I looked up, I thought I saw a dark figure moving between a couple of the trees. There are only six trees in the entirety of the cemetery, and they aren't well-lived enough to hide a person between their sand dried leaves. I stabbed my shovel into the ground hard so that it remained upright, and crept towards the trees. When I got there, I saw no one. I let out a large breath which I didn't even know I'd been holding in, and turned around, where I was met with my own shovel blade hitting me square in the face.

When I woke up, I thought I had gone blind. All I saw was darkness. I moved my hands up to feel my face to ensure I had indeed opened my eyes, but before I could get them there, my nails struck a wooden surface directly above me. I paused, and then tried to sit up. I lifted my head no more than four inches before it struck the same wooden surface. I pushed my arms out to my side, and they hit the same textured wood that was above me. That's when I knew. I was in a casket.

"Hello?" I squeaked out, my hot breath reflecting off the lid of the wooden structure and hitting me back in the face. "HELLO!"

I moved my left hand into a fist and tried to get enough force behind it to hit the lid, but when I did so, a trickle of dirt fell directly into my mouth. It didn't take me long to figure it out. The breath reflecting back at me meant I was no longer exposed to the cold air for it to dissipate. The dirt falling through the lid. I was buried alive. Most likely in one of the graves I had already dug. I screamed and screamed for what seemed like hours, before my throat became hoarse and I decided to try and conserve some air.

"So this is it."

I started to talk out loud to myself in an effort to calm my nerves and the dread I was feeling in every fibre of my being.

"Buried alive by a serial killing cemetery owner. I should've just stayed in San Francisco, done what Seacroft wanted and then gone somewhere else."

The confined space was now beginning to get to me. But not nearly as much as the other voice did.

"Yeah, that would have been a much better idea, Reg. Then again, you always were oblivious to the obvious."

If I'd have had anywhere to go, I'd have jumped about a mile off the ground. As it was, I smacked my head on the casket lid again, and this time drew blood. I could feel the damp stickiness as it trickled down from above my eye. I recognised that voice, but it couldn't have been. It wasn't possible.

"Who said that?" I asked to the wooden surface in front of me.

"You know damn well who said it Reg. Stop being so fucking stupid and look at me."

No. No this was not happening. I'd obviously started to hallucinate from lack of air. Either that or I was already dead and seeing and hearing things. No. This was *not* happening. But then I felt eyes on me, and realised it very fucking much was happening. I turned my head to the left, and somehow, some way, the left side of the coffin was gone, and laying alongside me in an open expanse of dirt… was Ralph.

8

"How the fuck are you here?"

Given the situation facing me, I guessed the theory that I was dead or dying and the lack of air was making me see apparitions, was probably the correct one. Not sure exactly why I would picture Ralph squished in his own coffin though. To be honest, I weren't sure entirely why I'd be imagining this treacherous bastard at all, let alone in the neighbouring casket.

"Well Reg, I figured you could use some help. Graveyard shift is much easier when there's two of you. Then again, I told you that years ago. Now look at you. Buried in a grave you dug just hours earlier, with nobody on the staff to come rescue you."

Even in the cramped conditions, I began to flail about angrily. While it was true that Ralph had offered to help out part time, I didn't exactly want to be reminded of that fact at this specific time.

"Look, I don't need fuckin' dead traitors tellin' me 'I told ya so' right now. So either kill me, or help me get outta here."

Ralph started to giggle.

That *really* pissed me off.

I was about to launch a full tirade of abuse his way, but then I noticed, although it was coming from his direction, the giggle was not him. I pressed myself up against the wooden lid and looked past him, where I saw the dirt had expanded the void and alongside Ralph in another casket... was Jean.

"You really are your worst enemy, Reg, you know that?"

Her voice, even after all these years, melted my heart. She looked exactly as she had the day she died. Before Ralph killed her, of course. Beautiful eyes shining a sapphire colour, the little twinkle still there despite the lack of light here. She was wearing the necklace I gave her as a birthday gift six months prior. I'd never dreamed one day she's be killed by it. She seemed to notice me looking and replied almost telepathically.

"This was always my favourite gift anyone gave me," she said, running her fingers through the chain. "Not just because it came from you, but because of how you got it."

Yet another memory seared into the back of my mind. The folks of Crossroads in general were kind folk. But some of them were more discriminating than others. The man I purchased the necklace from had constantly reminded me during the act of shopping that he was surprised one of 'my kind' could afford such a thing. It didn't matter that I'd worked my ass off to save up enough money to buy the thing, he only saw the colour of the hand holding them money and assumed I'd gotten it by ill means. I showed him though. I spread the word of his little racist mouth and all those kind and loyal to my family stopped buying his wares. He confronted me in the street one day calling me all manner of nasty things. I baited him, let him carry on his verbal diarrhoea, until the Sheriff emerged from his office long enough to hear some of the accusations and slurs, and then I knocked his ass to the floor. Sheriff said it was self defence and slammed him into a jail cell. He was let out of course, after all he was a rich white man. But he was never that outspoken again. I told Jean and Ralph the whole story. Kept calling me the Obsidian Ranger. Jean's way of calling me a black jewel without saying the word 'black.' Always worried she would offend me. I think that's why I fell in love with her. She was so considerate to other people and honest and trustworthy. That's why it hurt so much the night I found her with Ralph.

"You know, I regret how things turned out that night, but you had to know seeing you two together hurt me."

That's when the confused look spread across both of their dead faces. They looked at each other, and then the confusion was replaced with worry. I'd almost say terror.

"Reg, what are you talking about? We weren't together. You remember what happened right?"

Ralph had urgency in his voice that I couldn't quite understand. His eyes were wide and Jean's behind him, matched in their gaze.

"I remember watching Jean go into your house. I remember your sister telling me that she was in your bedroom. I remember walking in and seeing you fucking her on your parents' bed! Yes I remember what happened!"

My anger had raised my temperature even more, and the confined space wasn't helping. I could feel my head getting lighter, and the sweat pooling beneath me. But Ralph and Jean kept looking back and forth from each other like I had just shot their god damn puppy or something. It was Jean who told me. It was her that made me question every single thing about that night, and forget being buried alive, Seacroft's job offer, everything.

"Reg... Ralph doesn't have a sister."

9

Fifteen years earlier

It had been a long time since I'd thought about this night, and in less than a month, I'd been forced to relive it twice. Except I hadn't gotten it right the first time. I saw that now. But this wasn't me reliving the memory like I had done in the company of Samuel Seacroft.

I was there.

I stood in the corner of Ralph's house, not fire from the fireplace, and in the opposite corner, stood the ghosts of Ralph and Jean.

"What is this?" I asked, but they both held their fingers to their lips, and directed me to watch.

There was a knock at the door, and the Ralph of fifteen years ago strolled along the floor to answer it. As it swung open, there was Jean, looking just as the apparition did now. He kissed her on the cheek as he always did, but she did not run into his arms or anything of the sort.

"Evening Miss Jean, what brings you here?" he said with a slightly drunken slur.

"I was hoping I could talk to you about a gift I was thinking of getting for Reg. Gotta be secret though, so you can't tell him!"

Ralph chuckled to himself.

"Why don't you just tell him already, the guy is crazy about you just the same. Put him out of his misery!"

Jean blushed and moved in, closing the door behind her.

"I want to, but I always get the feeling he's not quite ready. Like he's holding part of himself back."

Ralph nodded. He knew I had been hurt in the past by a woman who turned out to work in the brothel above the saloon. She'd made me feel like such a fool, but I was too young to be flirting with women let alone wanting more, so I took it hard. Jean was different.

"So what is it you're thinking of getting him?"

Jean looked around, ensuring they were alone. That's when I realised something. The girl who had answered the door to me, was not here. I moved to ask the question, but apparition Jean simply shook her head, so I stayed quiet and continued to watch.

"Let's go in there," she pointed towards the parent's bedroom.

"Okay, I'll go make us some tea and be right in."

Jean nodded and hurried into the bedroom, and it

was only then I noticed the small pouch she was carrying. Ghostly Jean spoke to me for the first tie.

"I'd already bought it. I was too excited. But I wanted Ralph's opinion because it would be a pretty personal thing to give to someone, and I was worried you'd say no. It wasn't the done thing for a lady to ask. But it felt… right."

My stomach plummeted and I swear my fucking heart dropped into my boots. *It wasn't the done thing for a lady to ask.* Oh god.

Ralph lit the fire on the stove and placed the battered metal teapot on the flame, and it was after he had stopped rustling things around, I could hear the noises coming from the bedroom. Ralph heard too, and moved towards the doorway. His face turned to one of horror, and he sprinted inside. There was a loud bang as he was thrown back against the door, which slammed hard. I wanted to run in and go check, but ghostly Ralph held his arm across me to stop that action. Instead he spoke quietly.

"When I went inside, I saw him. And I saw her. I saw what they were doing. I couldn't believe it. In my own house, without a care in the world. My Eloise."

If my stomach could have sunk even lower, it would have. But Ralph's story was interrupted by the small sound of breaking glass near the kitchen area. As I watched, staggered, the woman who I had seen in the house that night, climbed in through the window. She glanced around and started looking for things. As I watched on, she picked up Ralph's pocket watch, and other valuable trinkets from around the room, and stuffed them into her pockets. She moved towards the bedroom door and flinched at the commotion going on in there, and moved towards the table.

Then came the knock at the door. *My knock*.

The woman's eyes darted towards the door and then behind her towards the bedroom. She moved cautiously over to the door and opened it. And there I was. Maybe she thought it was a distraction, or a good cover for what she was doing, but she pointed me in the direction of the bedroom door, and started rifling through a pile of knitting on the dining table. She hadn't been making scarves, she'd been *stealing* them. I knew what came next in my mind, but then I realised that in fact I had no idea what happened. My memory was fuzzy, I couldn't remember the faces I saw at the time, nor the noises exactly, and I'd already been proven wrong about the extra woman. Which meant one of two things.

Seacroft knew about this woman and was lying... or...

I soon got my answer.

As the me of the past opened the bedroom door, the previously fuzzy pictures became crystal clear. I saw everything without interruption. No longer was I looking through the haze of the bottom of a whiskey bottle and with young eyes. I saw the truth.

On one side of the bedroom, I saw a bloodied and beaten Ralph, trying to tend to Jean who was sporting a cut above her left eye, and a swollen lip. Ralph had removed his shirt to try and stop the bleeding, but he looked almost unconscious himself. The couple on the bed, however, were not stopping in their activities. And it was the *true* couple on the bed which horrified me.

Samuel Seacroft was fucking Eloise.

This was not an assault, she was *loving it*. My mind raced with such ferocity and confusion, probably from the whiskey, that I must have seen the initial faces of Ralph and Jean and projected them onto the couple in the bed. There was a flash of light, and we were back in the main area of the house. Jean was pleading with me, and I didn't hear it. Ralph was screaming at Seacroft, but was batted away. And I didn't hear any of it. And then the final moments.

Ralph swung to hit a now clothed and visible Samuel Seacroft, but he ducked down and caught Jean by mistake. Seacroft in his efforts to strike back, missed and hit Eloise instead, who ran out of the house in tears, not quite as fully dressed as the night air may have demanded. But I had completely blacked out Seacroft's presence. I pushed Ralph down onto Jean, and I watched as his hands spread out to try and push back up, but his hands were pressing down on the edges of Jean's necklace. *I* was forcing *him* to strangle her. And then, the rest is how I remembered it. I kicked the chair the woman was sat on, broke off its leg, and as she rolled under the table, I beat Ralph's skull in with it. Future me watched as the woman in question snuck out into the night, the knitted scarf around her neck, and both Ralph and Jean were dead.

And I'd killed them.

10

I don't remember exactly how long I was out for, but the squawking sound of a crow on the tree branch high above me woke me from my slumber. My fingers were in agony. As I tried to pull myself to a seated position, I screamed in pain. My fingernails were gone. Splintered and bloody, and there were hundreds upon hundreds of splinters and wood fragments protruding from the wounds. My hands were caked in mud, and my toes were throbbing. I turned around and saw what looked as if a beast had erupted from the ground. It was the grave I had been dumped in. I couldn't piece it together, but luckily, my ghostly friends had not abandoned me.

"You went at that thing like a crazed wildebeest."

Ralph's voice now had a tone of regret about it. I glanced over to the base of the tree and saw both him and Jean propped against it.

"I-… I'm so…"

I couldn't form the words, I couldn't even fathom the reality of what I had done. My rage was still present but lurking just behind it was an ocean wave of swirling devastation. I began wrenching the splinters and wood shards from the ends of my fingers, the blood dripping into the dirt and sand beside me as if someone had left a broken tap to drip. Then I noticed my chest was heaving and my breaths were coming in sharp and painful splintering rasps. I knew they were right. Learning the truth about what happened that night, and what I had done had driven me to the point of insanity and I had broken and clawed my way out of that hole like an animal. I slumped forwards, the blood continuing to drip from my fingers, and sobbed. The tears made little dust clouds as they hit the ground, and moments later, I felt a cool hand on my shoulder. It was Jean.

"It wasn't your fault Reg. You didn't cause all this."

The tears burst out of my eyes and I tried to argue, after all I had just seen the truth before those same eyes.

"Wasn't my fault? I KILLED YOU! I was so consumed by what I saw that I battered my best friend to death for trying to help you! In doing that, I killed you too! I loved you, and I killed you!"

The rage and the anger swirled within me. I began pounding my bloodied fists into the ground. I felt one finger break then another, and a third, before a stronger but equally as cool hand stopped my left fist in mid air, and slowly closed over it. Ralph stood looking at me with pity.

The Graveyard Shift

"We saw what happened too, Reg. Afterwards. When we realised there was no heaven or hell for us to go to. It was replayed to us, like we were stuck in a time loop. We saw your face, we saw the confusion, and we saw what you saw. That's when we knew it wasn't your fault."

"*It was his fault.*"

Jean's voice came out in a hiss, and her cool hand almost warmed with the heat of her words. It scared me a little, I gotta say. Having a ghost talk to you is one thing, but feeling one get angry is a whole other experience, let me tell you.

"Seacroft."

Ralph spoke as if he had spat out a bullet from his mouth. The hatred was clear. Obviously being dead doesn't alleviate your emotions.

"Who was he?" I asked through short breaths as I eased my breathing into some kind of normal rhythm.

"He'd just arrived in town, a week or so before. Came over from England, thinking he was lord of the whole fuckin' country. Caught Eloise in the general store one day, and started spouting some fancy big words, and before the day was out, they were screwin' up against the back of the barn at Silverton's place.

I never saw him until the night we were in the saloon toasting the engagement. Saw him glance across towards the exit before we ordered our third bottle. Neither of them had any scruples about what they did. At least I got to tell her exactly how it felt… and punish her."

That last part sent chills through my very soul. I was only just coming to terms with the fact that Seacroft's entire story about the extra woman being his wife was complete bullshit. He had heard that I'd come to San Francisco and he singled me out personally. For what? Punishment for ruining his night with my best friend's fiancee? But I was pretty sure I just heard Ralph tell me a ghost got revenge. There's a lot of ghosts around the Old West I am absolutely sure of it, but the thought of them getting revenge was just a step too far for my imagination to cope with.

"What exactly do you mean by punish her?"

I cursed myself the second the question left my lips, but figured the pain in my extremities was enough punishment for gaining more details I didn't need to know about.

"We're kinda stuck here, on our own little graveyard shift. Well, we can move between here where you buried us, and my old place where I was killed. But just a few weeks later, Eloise showed up. Here. Dead."

Jean walked over to him and planted a hand on his shoulder, feeling it necessary from the look now on his face to take over the story.

"Seacroft was just discovering that he had a taste for blood, and when it came out about us two being killed, Eloise was worried that the deaths would be pinned on them, and so she went to Samuel, who in turn slit her throat from ear to ear, and hung her up in the Silverton barn to drain out like a pig. The Sheriff found her, but as he couldn't get in touch with her family, he kept the matter quiet, and buried her here himself. Over there."

Jean pointed at a blank space between two gravestones, that had a noticeable divot. There was indeed a casket under that ground. And it had clearly been a grave dug by an amateur, because it had already begun to subside. Weirdly, that made me take a bit more pride in my craft and I felt a smile creep onto my face, even though this was the most inappropriate moment. Fuck it. I was talking to two dead people. And then two became three.

"I was next."

We all turned to look towards the opposite side of the unmarked grave for Eloise, and there she was, standing there with her stolen scarf wrapped around her neck.

"You."

She nodded and Jean introduced her.

"Reg, this is Penny. She was the one stealing from Ralph's that night. He'd bought her family home, and evicted them. They lived out on their own, nearer to the sea, and he wanted to start building some kind of town there. Even had the balls to name it after the farm."

"Wealdstone."

The singular name which flowed through Penny's lips elicited more emotion and her ghostly cheeks became stained with tears.

"But how did Ralph punish Eloise's ghost?" I asked again, trying to take in all this information, acutely aware the sun was rising on the horizon.

"I helped him," Penny whispered, barely audible over the now light breeze whipping up around us.

"Penny's mum was a witch. Well, sort of. She practiced occult magic, spells, rituals, that sort of thing. Seacroft's eviction tipped Penny's parents over the edge and they both took part in a blood pact. They took their own lives together. Then Seacroft found out Penny had been in Ralph's house that night too, and killed her just for extra measure."

I couldn't help but notice through all of this, the higher the sun rose, the fainter my friend's silhouettes became. It was as if the sun was erasing them from existence. I felt my time running out.

"Okay, then what?" I blurted quickly, trying to speed things up.

"Penny helped Ralph conjure a spell to banish a spirit to a place called the Void. A place of eternal darkness and concentrated evil. Without a heaven or a hell, it is the only place for souls or demons to go."

I had nothing to say.

"She screamed when she went."

Ralph's voice was wistful. The seeming perverse joy he had taken and the reminder he had cast her away was gone. This was my friend, the same one who had stood by me since I was a small boy. He did not take joy from Eloise's suffering. He was still Ralph, even now.

"Reg," Jean spoke. "We don't have much time, and we need to tell you what to do."

I had completely forgotten that it was likely

Seacroft who put me here in the first place, and I had to stop him.

"How do I find him?" I asked them all.

"He still intends to build Wealdstone, Reg. You have to go to Penny's old farm and confront him. He's going to keep killing, and he's going to make money from it. All of it. He's already wealthier than any land owner here, and once he becomes the builder of a new city, he's going to be unstoppable."

I nodded slowly. They were telling me what I already knew. Samuel Seacroft had to die.

"But I have no weapons, no forms of protection or anything!" I screamed out.

It was Penny who stepped forward. She spoke with a newfound determination. After all she had as much reason to want him dead than any of us.

"Go to the Silverton place. There are weapons in the barn. A lot of them. There's someone there who will help you. She tried to help me, but I was too stupid to listen."

As the sun rose over the top of the trees, the three of them faded away from view. Jean spoke one last sentence to me as her eyes vanished from my gaze.

"We'll always be here for you, Reg."

PART II

PART TWO - DANIELLA

11

"No, not like that!"

Jesus, I swear it never used to be this difficult to get good help. I knew I was now stuck in the arse end of nowhere both in terms of time period, and location, but surely they all couldn't be this stupid. There were good people in Crossroads. Well, *this* version of Crossroads anyway.

I watched as the two teenagers wobbled on the rickety ladders I had found in the barn, but finally managed to lift the giant cast iron letter 'S' onto the hooks they'd hammered into the wood the day before. That in itself had been a right fucking task. Still, if I was going to live in this time, I had to play my part. And most definitely try and stay out of history's way.

It has now, at the time of writing this, been eight months since I was thrown back in time from the year 2026, and landed on my ass in the dirt. But that's what you get for tangling with a Yellow Demon, I guess. I'd been convinced I could get back. Committed four years of my life to the cause, even enlisting the help of the ever mysterious Deanna. I did have to admit, travelling back through time, meeting an immortal being, and then learning about supernatural creatures living even in the 1800's was a bit of a blend of various TV shows, and *Back to the Future* vibes. Of course, I can say this to you readers, because by the time you find this... I guess... journal? You'll be back in good old modern times.

When Deanna found me on the side of the road, and told me all about her, she gave me a ride to San Francisco. I figured I'd be better able to explore exactly what technology of the time was like, what avenues were open to me, and had hoped they had better resources for telling me if and when Wealdstone might actually be constructed. Sadly, I had underestimated just how young a place Wealdstone was. The construction was not even mentioned. No plans, no blueprints, nothing. But I knew about Crossroads. I knew about the special geomagnetic energy beneath the place. That's when I bumped into that English cunt Samuel Seacroft. He'd just bought the main cemetery. Yeah because why would you not buy a huge plot of land full of dead people?

I was looking for a job to try and earn my way. Even in the late eighteen-hundreds, you can't get shit done without cash. He tried to pick me up in a bar when I managed to grab a day shift for a quick buck. I told him that he wasn't my 'type' and he lost interest for a while. Then I noticed that look he had. It was a look I'd seen many times before across several realities. That's when he offered me the job on the graveyard shift. Said it came with accommodation, and a good income. Said they were always looking for new staff as the turnover was quite high because of the hours. I told him I'd think about it, but when I ignored him, each time I managed to grab a shift at the bar, he would harass me, and each time it would be a sterner look in his eye when I'd turn him down. After about a month picking up regular work in the bar and getting good tips, I was actually making decent money.

Then I went to my rented room a few streets away after work one night, and found the place had been ransacked. Nothing was taken, just a bunch of shit destroyed. I raged for hours about it, but then figured it must have been Seacroft flexing his muscles. I righted the bed, grabbed my hunting knife, shoved it under my pillow and went off to sleep. The next day I went to head to work, but the bar wasn't there. Burned in an intense fire overnight. The owner, Hal, was killed. Burned alive in his sleep. Instantly, I was grateful that when he offered me a room above the bar, I'd turned him down. I needed more privacy than that would allow.

And then I saw him.

Samuel Seacroft was standing on the corner of the street, swinging some sort of cane around in his left hand, whistling a happy tune, smiling at me. Now this being me, naturally I stormed over to him, and grabbed him by the throat. That's when I knew he was dangerous.

"Tut, Tut Miss Silverton. We wouldn't want anything to happen to that pretty face of yours would we? Or that charmingly attractive lady you were seen arriving here with."

I knew Deanna could handle herself. She'd left a while back and while I was ninety-percent certain she was out of San Francisco by now, there was something about this man which said his reach went beyond the city limits. I let him go, swore I'd never work for him, and walked away. The very next day, I headed back to Crossroads. It was at this point that I gave up any notion of returning to my own time, and began scouring the area. As it turned out, there was a series of properties that had lain in waste and ruin for decades and there were no surviving family members to claim them. The lots were put up for auction, and I used all the money I had to buy the one furthest out from the main streets. I figured I'd name the place after a name I recognised, but nobody else would. At least not for over a hundred years or so. I thought about the people I'd left behind and the challenge they must have faced, and I named the land the Silverton property. I adopted the surname myself back in San Francisco, of course. Mostly for anonymity purposes, but I also felt some kind of guilt over the way my presence had broken up the marriage of a couple I knew. I adopted the name as a sort of tribute. Guess it sounds stupid to you.

After I'd spent a month or so doing the place up and

The Graveyard Shift

picking up shifts in the saloon here, I had an evening where I just sat out on the porch, drinking what the people of Crossroads called their finest beer (what I wouldn't give for a refrigerator) and contemplating life in general. It was after this reflective evening, I decided to venture into the post office and make a rather unusual request. I'd written a letter to Kristin Silverton, somebody who I had wronged before coming here, and I apologised for everything, told her what happened and told her that there was no hope of me getting back to them, so I was going to live my life here, and make the best of it. I told her that I hoped she could find happiness, sealed it up, and wrote the address to the mansion we had lived in on the envelope, hoping the address would be the same as in my reality. The guy at the counter was the most confused I had ever seen a person. He was a nice looking guy, maybe early to mid-thirties, and one of the few black people I had come across. They seemed to suffer quite extreme treatments in all time periods, as I was learning. That was another thing that made my blood boil, but there's a lot of that lately, so I'll get on with it. He and his manager promised me the letter would be delivered to the address requested after the correct number of years had passed, and I left, much to the bemusement of the young man who had welcomed me into the post office at the start. I never forgot that guy, mostly because I liked his attitude, and his quick wit resonated with me. I often thought how much of a joy he would have been to fight with in the future. It wasn't until a few weeks later, after I had started to mingle with the locals more, that I found out he was also the town's gravedigger. Apparently the older residents who used to look after the place passed on, and now he did it all on his own. Good on him, I remember thinking. Night is much more peaceful and the quiet is welcoming.

It was also, however, around this time that I learned the reason my property had been abandoned around fifteen years previously, was because they found a young woman murdered in the barn. Throat slit, and hung up to drain like an animal. And *that* led me to investigations, which led me to the truth that the person behind her death was most likely Samuel Seacroft. I couldn't delve too deep into the matter because I knew from my brief time in San Francisco that he was a dangerous man, and whilst I had fought far more deadly and powerful people and entities than him, right now, I was in a time without any semblance of technology from where I came from, and most importantly, I didn't have my team. I had learned from speaking with the locals that Seacroft had been here around fifteen years before, fresh off the boat from England. People didn't seem to like speaking about him much. It came to light that he had bought the farm of a local family, very close to the location I knew the main street of Wealdstone would one day stand, and evicted them. To be honest, the thought of Samuel Seacroft being the man who founded the town I loved made me feel physically sick. The fact that he had seemingly followed me back to Crossroads didn't help either.

The Graveyard Shift

While I didn't have the modified bullets, faster loading and firing weapons, or the enchantment of a sorceress to help me, I was able to get my hands on weapons of this time far more easily than in my own. Within just a few weeks, I was able to barter or buy over twenty guns and firearms, countless ammunition, and had several custom blades made by the local blacksmith. I decided to keep them in a hidden section of the barn. Then one day, I found a young woman trying to break in. She told me her name was Penny and it was in fact her family who Seacroft had evicted almost fifteen years ago. It was only then that I realised this girl was in fact dead.

Given my previous experience with the paranormal, which is extensive, I was surprised I had not picked up on the fact I was talking to a spirit sooner. She told me how she had died not far from here, but her energy was able to follow one of the geomagnetic currents beneath the ground. She was under the impression she could arm herself because even in death she was afraid of Seacroft. He had killed her to tie up loose ends from the events surrounding Eloise's death. She told me of incantations she knew and practiced in memory of her mother, and I found her devotion even though she was no longer living, honourable. Penny visited me often, and on occasion, she taught me how to use some of these spells her mother had taught her. One of them in particular, helped me erect a ward against a nasty clan of cowboy vampires that wandered into town last Christmas. They couldn't get onto my land, and rather than move on, they decided to try and find out why that was.

It had been excellent firing practice.

But I knew, that my ultimate goal would have to be Samuel Seacroft's downfall. I needed time to prepare and if possible, an ally or two, preferably living to help me. Thankfully I didn't need to wait long. As the boys who hung the iron letter over the barn entrance were leaving, another man was walking down the track towards my house. I felt the smile spread across my face as his features came into view.

I knew I always liked that guy from the post office.

12

"How do you know Seacroft?"

Reginald was a striking man indeed. He had not said much upon his arrival, but he did not seem too disturbed by the fact I had been semi-expecting him after my conversations with Penny. Part of me found myself captivated by his piercing brown eyes, despite the fact that I would never have spent time in a man's bed if I was paid all the gold in the world. Well... maybe I would if that happened, but you get my point. I answered his question by telling him all about my run ins with the slime of a man in San Francisco, and he surprised me by telling me a similar story. The confirmation of Seacroft being a killer still came as a slight surprise even though I had suspected him. The vast number of corpses he had left behind was the part that surprised me.

"That girl up at the cemetery told me you had weapons. A lot of weapons. That true?"

Reginald's directness was beginning to snag on the very edge of my comfort levels. I appreciated getting to the point, but he seemed oblivious to the most polite of manners. I suspected spending the night in a freshly dug grave and being helped out by spirits would have that effect on a man.

"Yeah. I stockpiled since I arrived here. Figured I had to start from scratch seeing as how I arrived here with nothing."

I stopped myself very quickly when I remembered I had left out the part where I had travelled back from the 2020's. I might not have wanted to get stuck here, but I was also conscious of the threat to changing history. For all I knew, me simply being here was already screwing history beyond repair, but there was also the possibility that I was in yet another reality as well as the past. Quantum Mechanics always did give me a headache. Then a thought occurred to me. Reginald had spent much more time with Seacroft than I had. Granted only a few days, but I only spent minutes at a time with him. I wondered if there may be… more, to his blood thirst.

"Reginald…"

"Call me Reg, Ma'am."

I'd never been called ma'am before, but I had to admit, I liked the way it sounded. Nobody had called me ma'am since I arrived, but I felt like I was in the company of a very kind and respectful gentleman.

"Reg, in the time you spent around Samuel, did you notice anything… unusual?"

The Graveyard Shift

Reg laughed, and I even smiled at the sound of that. What was wrong with me?

"You mean besides the rotting corpses he left in my bedroom, the pushing me into an unmarked grave and burying me alive, and his desire to build a massive town in the middle of fuckin' nowhere?"

"Well, yeah."

He laughed again and shook his head.

"No Miss Daniella, I did not."

Well it was worth an ask. He could of course just be your usual run of the mill serial killer. I don't ever remember there being a Samuel Seacroft mentioned in the history books around the birth of Wealdstone, but then again would I have looked at it that deeply? Either way, I was going to kill the man. So much for the potential timeline damage.

"The reason I ask is that there are some more… unusual people out there. How much do you know about the supernatural, besides ghosts?"

That caught his attention.

"You mean like vampires and shit?"

I nodded, leaning forward. Reg turned his head left to right, as if checking nobody else was overhearing or eavesdropping on our conversation.

"My brother once told me he thought he saw some huge wolf man lurking around on the outskirts of Crossroads once. I said he was probably drunk and seeing things, but I heard whispers others saw it too."

A wolf man? I personally hadn't encountered any werewolves either in my time or this one. So far, just the few vampires, and the ghost of Penny. But I suppose it could be true. I of course knew of their existence, confirmation of which I wasn't sure Reg could handle, but I chanced it anyway.

"Werewolves are common in the US. Not as common as vampires mind you. Had to dispatch a whole bunch of those thirsty fuckers at Christmas time. Felt good to get back in the saddle again."

It wasn't physically possible for Reg to turn white, but his expression matched the face of a person shocked to their core.

"You mean he was right?" he blurted out.

I nodded and let out a slight chuckle. I had been dealing with this kind of shit for decades so I sometimes forgot to other people it was all still new.

"It's kinda what I do. I've hunted vampires, demons, yellow demons specifically, pain wraiths, phantom wraiths. Even met a White Falcon once."

If I didn't know any better, I'd say Reg's internal hard drive had just crashed. Once his brain had rebooted, he seemed to focus less on those details and more on the end result.

"Can you kill 'em?"

"The scary shit? Or Seacroft."

"Yes."

I couldn't help but smile.

"I can kill anything."

13

The first thing I had to do was train Reg on how to use some of these weapons. For someone who claimed to be a gravedigger, he was incredibly well presented and not at all what I would've expected. His clothes were old, even for these times, but were immaculate. I later learned they had been passed down to him by his father. He certainly had the cowboy look more than the guy who dug holes in the ground at night for a living. Either way, a gun was not a shovel, and Reg admitted he had not been given cause to use a firearm much.

I'd had one of the local kids build me a more advanced version of a rig for shooting cans. Seven pikes of wood planted in the dirt about six feet apart from each other and standing around seven feet tall. At the top of each spike, I planted a hessian sack stuffed with various materials. Most were hay, some were dirt, and for realism, I filled two with meat. I made a note not to tell Reg which ones they were, but decided he would shoot those last. He had only killed by accident with his bare hands. He had never actually killed someone with a shot. He had to see what that might look like.

The first weapon was a rifle, and boy did he miss the target. In fact in the field behind my land, I heard several horses rear up and let out cries of fear, or perhaps anger. My neighbour would be on my ass for that, I was sure. But for now, honing the aim would be the priority.

"Reg, hold the butt of the gun against your shoulder blade and look down the line of the rifle, nuzzle the gun against your cheek. Pick the third target on the left, and get your breathing controlled."

He was a good student. He followed every instruction, silently, but accurately.

"Good, now when you're ready to fire, breathe out and as you do, pull the trigger."

BANG!

The third hessian bag was struck slightly off centre, but enough to send a huge plume of dust and fragments of hay up into the air. The celebration on my part was very happy and I patted Reg on the back. He, however, did not move from his stance or relax. He kept the weapon in the same position, and with his free hand, reloaded the rifle, never taking his eyes off the target. As he sent his second shot across the field, it hit the bag dead centre, and struck the wooden stake behind it, snapping it enough for the bag to fall to the ground. I

The Graveyard Shift

was now *very* impressed. For the next two hours or so, I moved him along the targets, running through the first five and then sending him back to the start with a different weapon. It was only after he noticed we weren't firing at the two targets on the end, that he moved towards me, and pointed at them.

"What about those two?"

There was a certain impatience in his voice. My planned secrecy about the contents of the final couple of targets had started to become less and less concealable as the hot sun had started to accelerate the meat's decomposition, and dark blood was now becoming visible through the hessian.

"I was saving those for last. They're designed to simulate the impact on a human, or humanoid creature. The sounds, the splatter, the feeling it gives you. There's no way to know how you're going to feel about taking a life deliberately, until you do it. It changes you."

Reg nodded, and took a deep breath and looked up at the sky as if he was reliving some kind of memory. Most likely a death, whether by his hand or another's.

"What did it feel like when you first killed someone?"

For some reason, the question caught me off guard. I had been expecting it but I couldn't formulate an answer immediately. So I relayed the story.

"I was nineteen. I was already aware of the dangers that lurked in Weald… my home town. My father had made sure of that. He had drummed into me how streets at night were no place for young girls alone. I didn't know he'd seen so-called creatures of the night, I just thought he meant perverts or killers. I was heading home from a date with a girl at my school. The night had gone well, and I'd been less shy than I worried I would be. We got around five minutes from my house and I figured we would say goodbye there, and I'd let her go on her way. When I turned back towards her I saw that her entire face had transformed. Her eyes were wider and hollow, her mouth had almost stretched across her face and her teeth were glistening, her top two canines stretched into fangs. She launched on me and pushed me off the edge of the road into a grove of trees. Her strength was overpowering, and I had done a lot of working out, but I was no match for her. Just as I felt her hot breath reach for my neck, my hands gripped onto an old piece of wood from a fallen tree. I heaved the pointed end upwards and it went right through her eye socket. I can still hear the pop of the eyeball, and her screams were almost like that of a banshee. Even with one eye gone, she came back at me. But she wasn't very smart and I'd become more confident, running on adrenaline. She yanked the wooden spike from her eye, and threw it to the ground, but it was closer to me than her. She stopped for a minute as she realised her mistake, but I'd already dove towards it, and as she leapt towards me, I raised it in the air. I closed my eyes and when I opened them, her body was turning to ash around me. It was my first encounter with a vampire."

Reginald listened to the story I gave, and his eyes became wistful. He stroked the black goatee beard on his chin as he contemplated something, but he spoke no words. His actions next were what made me realise that despite our short time together, he was ready.

He picked up a pistol from the table, lifted it without his gaze ever leaving my eyes and fired six rounds, his eyes never once flinching. When I gathered myself at the level of confidence he had displayed, I turned to look at the meat targets. There were three shots in each, top middle and bottom, blood slowly oozing out of all six. He lowered the gun, and examined it, turning it over in his hands.

"Yeah. This is the one. Now let's go kill that bastard."

PART III

PART THREE - REGINALD

14

Despite the slight pain in my wrist and my shoulder, I strapped the holster tight. The recoil on the weapons Miss Daniella had provided were much more powerful than I had expected, and despite the fact I now knew what the hell I was doing with a gun, the apparent confidence I had displayed to her was a sham. I heard her story about the vampire girl, and it just made me wanna rescue her. I can't explain why, and while I would never dare to presume a woman's age, that event must have been around twenty years previous. I simply aimed at where I thought one of the meat bags was and fired. All six were meant to go into target number six, but the recoil of the fast firing on my part jarred my hand to the left slightly, and three bullets ended up in meat bag number two. I had to admit, I was impressed they all ended up in near enough matching lines, but the smaller pistol felt good in my grip. It was manoeuvrable, and easier to conceal, unlike the larger rifle. The fact it could hold six bullets as opposed to one or two was also an advantage.

Miss Daniella was a strange one. I couldn't quite figure her out. She was forthcoming in all the details surrounding Seacroft and her intentions to dispatch him, but she was also very illusive. She had mentioned her school but not mentioned where it was she had grown up. She mentioned working out, which I assumed meant exercise of some sort. And there was something about her hair. She was an incredible beautiful woman, and I'd be lying if I said she didn't turn my eye, but her hair had what looked like different coloured roots. It was as if her long blonde hair was not naturally blonde at all. Then of course there was the realisation that it wasn't only people that walked our towns and cities. Every word she spoke to me made me wonder if Samuel Seacroft was indeed some kind of devil creature. Surely only something of Satan's own creation could be so evil and wicked to mercilessly kill all those people for fun.

Miss Daniella was kind enough to offer me her spare room so that we could keep our plans to ourselves and not arouse too much talk in the town. If anybody came by, we would say I was doing some work for her. People never thought twice when they were told that sentence. Something I always resented, but in this case would be a welcome excuse. In truth, Miss Daniella had four spare rooms. This property was large and the irony wasn't lost on me that she had acquired it in large part due to Seacroft's underhanded dealings. Neither was it lost on me that because of that, the preparations at this house would end him and his killings.

The first task was to find out where he would be. Well that was easy. The stupid English prick may as well have hoisted a huge iron 'dumb fucker at work' sign over his head. He'd travelled to the proposed site four miles away of this new Wealdstone place he so desperately wanted to build, and invited all the reporters in a one hundred mile radius to come and watch him break ground. As me and Daniella had discovered, Samuel Seacroft had been very busy indeed. This breaking ground ceremony was entirely for show. Two further miles to the west, he had already started construction on some kind of huge jetty which jutted out into the sea. I'd never been one for the ocean. It was peculiar in the States to have a desert town so close to the ocean, but there wasn't much about this place that wasn't irregular. We had cacti, ocean and snow in the winter. Not many places in the US that could claim that.

The next step was finding transport. It was a fairly short journey, but I had only ever borrowed horses, and Miss Daniella had lost her only horse when the vampires attacked her. Every penny she had was poured into the purchase and restoration of the now Silverton property, and the guns and ammo. I had a couple of friends in town who could possibly help, but I decided to go alone. I didn't want word getting around that we were travelling to the site of Wealdstone for fear Seacroft would hear. If he was human, he would certainly have a massive entourage, and if he was demonic, we didn't wanna force his hand. Surprise was all we had. While Miss Daniella worked with the local kids who helped her with some of her restoration work on the barn to patch up a broken old wagon she found, I ventured back into Crossroads to see a man about a horse.

Manny Santiago was both a friend and a bastard. I had known him most of my life, and he had fought beside me in many bar fights. But every so often, he would spy an opportunity to get one over on you for financial gain. It didn't happen often, but when it did, it fucking hurt like hell. But right now, he was the only one I could rely on to get hold of a horse for me. I'd stolen a horse from San Francisco to come back and for fear of getting caught upon my return, I'd set it free. Bit of a stupid fucking thing to do in hindsight, but here we were. Dusty and desperate. I knew Manny liked to frequent the ladies every Friday afternoon, so I decided to wait for him outside. He was a daytime user of the local establishment rather than a nighttime one. Oh no, you'd never catch Manny Santiago in a brothel after nightfall. That was when the Sheriff was looking the other way, and there were business dealings to be done. He was, however, like clockwork. At noon he would go inside, at one-thirty he would go across the saloon for a drink, and then at two-thirty he would head back for round two, exiting at three-thirty without fail.

Only this time, he didn't.

His horse was tied up outside the saloon, but he

The Graveyard Shift

wasn't inside, which meant he had to be in the brothel. At four, he still hadn't come out. I loathed going into places like this, but I didn't feel I had much choice. We would need everything in place by tonight, as me and Miss Daniella were eager to set out for Wealdstone the next morning. I was not prepared for what I would see when I opened the door.

Immediately, my foot slid away from me, and I had to grab hold of the door to keep myself upright. I knew what the liquid was before I laid eyes on it. Blood. And lots of it. This place had a triple door entry for privacy. With that in mind, nobody outside had seen this yet. If they had, there would have been an uproar. I looked back up from the pool of blood my boot was now a part of, and struggled to hold my breakfast in place.

There was broken glass everywhere, the stench of booze filled the air, mingled with that of shit, piss and blood. The madam of the place, Genevieve, was slumped backwards in a chair, three claw marks across her chest, and one along her throat. Directly in front of me was a group of body parts. I couldn't tell which parts belonged to who, but there were at least five arms, four legs, and definitely three heads. It looked like someone had chopped these girls up for firewood. The stairs to the rooms were in the far left corner, and it took all my balance to stop from sliding on my ass with all that blood around. The one fact I was trying not to focus on in all this mess was the fact that none of these women had died of gunshots or knife wounds. They'd been *chopped up*.

The stairs were fairly blood free, and I saw no other bodies as I reached the veranda which looked out over the downstairs like a mezzanine. All of the doors were closed except one. The room at the end of the corridor was open, and from inside, I could hear some kind of squelching sound. For the first time in my life, I was glad I'd armed myself. I reached into my black leather jacket and slid the gun from its holster, flexing my fingers on the grip before taking a firm hold. As I approached the door, the noises got louder, and I realised it wasn't a squelching sound, but a gargling sound that I was hearing. Like the sound of a man drowning in his own blood.

I took a deep breath and span round the door. Manny Santiago was being held about three feet off the ground, his feet kicking violently in the air, spasming out of his control. His blood was dripping beneath his feet onto the dusty wooden floorboards.

And Samuel Seacroft was eating his flesh.

For a minute, time seemed to stand still. The figure of Seacroft was unmistakable despite him having his back to me. The white suit, cane propped by the bed with its distinctive white serpent figurehead, and the silvery hair. My foot caught a nail in the floor and Seacroft flinched at the noise. His body shifted slightly, enough so I could see Manny's eyes still flickering, his mouth pouring with blood as it moved up and down instinctively, and the gaping flesh wound in the middle of his chest. As I took all this in, Seacroft turned his head towards me, but his face wasn't... complete.

His jaw had somehow become detached and opened like some god damn saloon door, and inside this hole were rows and rows of razor sharp teeth, almost rotating like a wheel. His eyes were black, and his moustache dripping with Manny's blood. His fingernails had morphed into some kind of talons too. That, I suspected was what had torn the ladies apart downstairs. I watched, frozen and unable to move as Seacroft dropped Manny's body to the floor with a sickening thump, and his face began to fold back into itself. His talons retracted back into his fingernails, and he took one step forward, his eyes shifting back and forth as if he was unable to decide what to do.

And then he *smiled* at me.

I didn't even get chance to raise the pistol past my waist before he charged at me. It felt like I'd been hit by a train. His shoulder slammed into my ribs and I barrel rolled backwards out of the door and slammed into the railings behind me. Seacroft didn't stop, and as he reached me, he leapt into the air, cleared the railings and plunged over the edge. I turned my neck as quickly as I could and saw him land on the welcome podium next to the madam's slashed corpse, splintering the wood with the force, and then he darted out into the daylight.

I stayed there dazed for a few minutes, before I decided it would be best if I left via the back entrance in case Seacroft decided to send the Sheriff my way to help cover his tracks. But even if he did, there was no way anyone could think this attack was made by a human. The violent and visceral nature of this was simply animalistic. As I walked out the back door, nursing my wounds, and wiping blood off the toe of my boot, I realised I at least had one answer to a pressing question.

Samuel Seacroft was definitely not human.

15

"Fuck."

Considering the graphic detail of what I had just told Miss Daniella, her reply was somewhat restrained. I still wasn't used to the fact that creatures like this were the norm for her previously. I still wasn't clear on where that was exactly, but there were more pressing matters to attend to. Like the blowing off of Samuel Seacroft's skull.

"So what the hell do you think he is?"

Miss Daniella had the expression of an incredibly concentrated thought process carved into her face. Occasionally, her eyes would dart left to right as if reading some imaginary book that I couldn't see. But whatever she was trying to search for must have eluded her, because a few moments later, she let out a long sigh and just shook her head as she lowered it.

"I can't remember half of the things I used to know

before I came here. It's almost like travelling back through time gives you a mental wipe of some…"

She stopped the second she realised what she had just admitted. I didn't process the words myself for a few moments. I was still thinking of the rows of pulsing teeth I'd seen tearing through Manny's flesh. But I was sure I'd heard her correctly.

Time Travel.

She attempted to move on, grabbing a shotgun and loading shells into the side, but I wasn't about to let this go.

"Y'all just said a bunch of shit that I can't process, so you best sit your pretty little ass back down and explain that shit to me… ma'am."

Despite everything, Miss Daniella smiled at me. I got the feeling that despite my occasional outbursts, she enjoyed the fact that I could be both gentlemanly and direct when called for. I, however, was not prepared for what she told me next.

I learned about how she had lost most of the people she loved to a creature called a Pain Wraith which from what I could gather was some angry ass ghost with a taste for blowing shit up. I learned that just as they'd recovered from that, some other angry son of a bitch called Monarch who was some kind of body snatching demon had pretty much finished off her friends and family before throwing her through a mystical doorway at *her* version of Crossroads, and she'd ended up somewhere near Eureka. Then she told me that all this took place in the twenty-first century, that she'd hooked up with a chick from an alternate dimension before being thrown back in time, and that she named the land the Silverton Ranch to kind of make up for screwing this young lady around. Oh and if that wasn't enough, when she did find herself in this time, she travelled with another woman for a while who was immortal.

I think I got all of that.

And you know what?

I didn't even question it.

I can usually tell when people are bullshitting me. There was only truth in her eyes. And after everything I had seen in the last week or so, who was I to argue that I was sat next to a time travelling badass cowgirl?

"You know, nobody else knows about that Reg. Except Deanna. But I remember your face the day I came into the post office to send that letter. Now you know why."

I hadn't forgotten that day, after all it was quite the unusual request to make. I didn't want to ask what was in the letter as I didn't feel it was my place. Miss Daniella was entitled to her privacy. She was lucky others didn't know about her preference for the fairer sex round here, though. They'd have tried to recruit her into the brothel as an extra special attraction. The men in Crossroads didn't tend to have much in the way of scruples. Of course now they had no brothel left either after the state Seacroft left it in.

"You know Miss Daniella, I've never wanted much from my life. The one thing I truly desired, Jean, was taken from me. All I've wanted to do since then is just stay in a quiet life, and work the graveyard shift at the cemetery. But you've brought this whole new energy with you from wherever it is you've come from. And I think I like it. I mean how many folk can say they've battled demons and spoken to spirits? Well, in this time anyway."

She laughed and nodded her head, her blonde locks falling like a waterfall over her shoulder. But then her face turned more serious. She gripped the barrel of the shotgun and stood sharply. She slowly rose her gaze towards me, and a smile formed in the crook of her lips.

"Let's go hunt us down an asshole."

16

We saw the exterior shells of the buildings before we even reached the site for Wealdstone. Daniella signalled to stop, and we pulled up the horses, red dust billowing around us. The Sheriff hadn't noticed us sneak past earlier and unhitch them from the saloon. After all he had enough on his plate mopping up pieces of the clientele across the street. Daniella had suggested we approach from the back end of where the town would be to avoid the press and the immediate gaze of Samuel Seacroft. It was only going this way that we saw just how much of the town had already been constructed.

"What is all that?" I asked, still in awe of how so many structures could just pop up without anyone taking notice.

"That one there is going to be my favourite bar," she said, gesturing towards a medium sized structure in the middle of the row ahead of us.

"Priorities," I chuckled to myself. "I suppose telling me anything else is screwing with the timeline?"

Daniella tilted her head to the left and waved a so-so gesture with her hands.

"To be honest, most of this will be long gone and rebuilt five or six times over by the time I'm meant to be born, so it wouldn't mess with it as much as you might think."

You did have to admire Seacroft though. Targeting such a vast piece of land that it spanned the edge of the desert, and the edge of the coast would be an incredibly lucrative venture. Almost seemed like he was building his own private San Francisco out here.

"We'll head at him from the opposite end of where Main Street starts, and wait for the reporters to fuck off before we make our move."

Daniella jerked the reigns of her horse off towards what she'd called her favourite bar, and circled round the back of the building. It did seem to be one of the only ones almost fully constructed. Like I'd said… priorities. Towns needed three things to start up. Somewhere to drink, somewhere to fuck, and somewhere to sleep. In that order. Even Seacroft seemed to be following that line of reasoning. Opposite the unfinished bar was what looked like a complete copy of the brothel back at Crossroads. Clearly his visit there had been business as well as… lunch.

We dismounted our horses, and gave them a gentle pat to send them away. If they were spotted, our position would be known. Daniella led us inside the

The Graveyard Shift

shell of the bar, and we hunkered down beneath one of the empty window frames.

"Favourite bar, huh?" I asked as I took a swig of water.

She nodded.

"Yeah. It's called Sisko's. Place has been through some pretty rough times, but it's the one place in Wealdstone that never goes anywhere. It's weird to see it like this, but it still feels like home."

She ran her hands across the wooden edge of the lower wall, and I was sure I saw tears forming in her eyes, but she turned away as they moved to fall down her cheek. Her attention had been captured by movement outside. A cold shiver went down my spine as I saw where she was looking, and *what* she was looking at.

Half way down what would be Main Street, three burly men all wearing impeccable suits, were marching towards us, but their faces were fully open with their rows of circulating teeth on display for anyone to see. Slithers of drool fell from the flaps of skin that had unhinged to show off such a horrific image. It appeared our problems had just quadrupled. It appeared Seacroft was not alone. My fingers began itching against the butt of my twin pistols, but Daniella reached behind her and held my hands steady. She then gestured with her head at where the creatures were going.

Beside the brothel was what looked like an old mine shaft. Nobody had mined anything out here for generations, but nevertheless, this things were headed

93

down there. One by one they vanished down a tunnel out of view.

"Well," said Daniella, "I'm glad we brought the torches."

I wasn't.

I knew exactly what that meant, and while I was enjoying the heroic, grave digging cowboy battler of supernatural demons, the last thing I wanted to do right now was dive into a cave full of face-sucking monsters.

"Oh no. Absolutely not. I am not going into that dark ass tunnel with a bunch of demonic things with razor blades for faces."

I made my voice stern, and literally put my foot down, looking Daniella deep in the eyes, not breaking my stare once.

17

As we moved further down the entrance to the tunnel, I could feel water dripping down my neck from above. While we had brought torches with us, because of the weapons we were carrying, they were only small hand held versions. This meant the flaming rags were much closer to my bare skin than I would like, and I kept having to stop myself switching that and one of my pistols from hand to hand. Only holding one of my new favourite weapons made me feel off balance. I'd practiced the last few days with both, and now I felt almost lopsided. Miss Daniella had no troubles there. She had demonstrated how deadly she could be with a shotgun using just one hand back at the Silverton Ranch. If anything, I felt like her sidekick.

Ahead of us, I could see a faint light and heard the murmuring of voices. No, not voices. Growls? Whatever it was, it was getting closer and I felt my hand involuntarily tighten around the grip of my pistol.

Daniella pressed herself up against one side of the tunnel and gestured me forward until I reached her position, and we stopped. Although I didn't speak it out loud, I mouthed one word.

"Shit."

Just below us in a wide cavern that must have spanned a hundred feet across, there were exactly twenty-five open mouthed creatures, positioned in a perfect circle against the cavern walls. And whilst the rock in front of each of them appeared to be black or volcanic in appearance on first look, was most definitely not. A breeze from somewhere in the chambers blew the flames of one of the creatures' torches closer to the rock work which confirmed it was indeed a crimson red colour.

The walls were quite literally dripping with blood.

And then I saw where it was coming from.

Each creature's head was moving rapidly from side to side in little jerking motions. They were feeding on a person. Twenty-five individuals were hanging from a ledge above them, and each creature was feasting on them like they were prime rib. Claws held the bodies in place, and each face was in a different state of either decay or integrity. I felt the bile rise in my throat but swallowed it back down. Daniella remained hard faced. I couldn't tell if this was the usual for her, or whether she was equally disturbed by this as I was. I hoped I'd never get to a place where this became normal for me. Then again, I'd have to live through this first.

And then he walked out of the shadows and stood in

The Graveyard Shift

the centre of the group. Samuel Seacroft was now sporting a freshly laundered, or entirely new version of what had become his trademark look. A pristine white suit, grey tie and his fingers shaped his trimmed grey moustache. Although to look at him, his hair was now almost as white as his suit. The man appeared to have aged a good ten years since I'd seen him munching his way through the brothel. We kept pressed tightly against the rocks, and Daniella gestured for us to dowse our torches. Upon Seacroft's appearance, the other creatures stopped feeding, and folded their mouths back into place one by one, their claws retracting as they did so. Seacroft nodded in approval and then addressed the room.

"My brothers, the time is almost upon us. We have been trapped in these caverns for far too long, and our time is almost at hand."

I would have called it a cheer, but it sounded more like a joint guttural roar came from each of the twenty-five in perfect synchronicity. Seacroft continued.

"The drifters and the weak have served us well in recent decades, but we shall hide in the shadows no more. We will build this town as a haven for our kind, and the humans will flock to these shores in their millions. We shall never risk starvation again!"

Another loud roar echoed around the cavern. Seacroft then moved to his left and took hold of one of the torches. He turned around to walk back the way he came, but stopped when he had illuminated what was hanging on the wall behind him. Daniella moved a hand across her mouth. Even she couldn't hide her disgust at what she saw. Hanging in chains on a rockface in front of Seacroft, was the tattered remains... of Samuel Seacroft.

At least, that's what it looked like. The face was the same, although aged and weathered, and it sported a white mane of long scraggly hair and a beard to match. The flesh ended at the top of the chest, and only skeletal remains existed from there on out. There appeared to be some kind of trough at the bottom of this strange altar, and in the light of Seacroft's torch, I could see it was blood. He placed the torch into a holder on the wall, and lowered his hand into the blood, lifting it up to his mouth and slurping hungrily at the liquid. Despite licking at it with such ferocity, none made it onto his perfect suit. When he turned to address the crowd once more, his eyes were now a crazy shade of red.

"Our father, MY father, has nourished me for longer than most of you have existed. He gave his life so that I may live and now I will lead you to the surface, and to your rightful place as rulers of these pathetic human creatures!"

The twenty-five now started stomping their feet on the ground, sending little plumes of dust into the air, which began to form a mist around the cavern, with it having nowhere to go. The stomping got louder and faster, and under the cover of this dust, Daniella led us across a short open space and into another hidden nook in line with Seacroft. It was at this moment that we got the answer to another one of our questions.

The Graveyard Shift

"Too long have we Lorengar been kept out of sight. It was hard for me to leave you, my brothers, but it was necessary to craft our path. I ventured as far as England to build the resources needed to do what must be done to ensure our freedom. Upon my return to the United States, I attempted to find ways for our species to breed. However, these human females are far too weak. And then my eventful excursion to San Francisco."

Samuel and the rest of the rabble began to laugh as if the funniest joke in the world had just been told. I looked at Daniella, and she shrugged back at me. At least she didn't have a fucking clue what this psycho was going on about.

"Who would have thought I would stumble across a cemetery full to the brim of fresh meat? These humans aren't as smart as they like to think, but preserving the dead, helped us no end. I do enjoy the tang of a high quality embalming fluid."

More laughter from the crowd, and this time it was Daniella who was struggling not to bring up her breakfast. But Seacroft wasn't done.

"Purchasing the land was easy enough, of course. With the old owner out of the way, it was simply a case of making an offer to the widow and carrying on with it. The people of San Francisco treated me well. Although, there were a few downsides when the staff of this graveyard shift discovered my activities and I had to deal with them. The loss of my Sergeant was also tragic. It always is when you lose a brother in arms. And then there were two others who caused me nothing but grief. Wasn't there Reginald? And of course the lovely Daniella."

My blood froze cold, as Seacroft slowly turned his head towards us, gesturing with his arm and looking right into my eyes. The crowd grew furious, and began stumbling over each other to launch towards us. After a second or two, Daniella snapped out of her trance and began firing into the crowd, hitting the nearest of these Lorengar things, blowing their heads clean off their shoulders. Yep. That seemed to do the trick. I pulled my second pistol from my rear holster and immediately felt balanced once more. I joined Daniella, covering her when she needed to reload, but the crowd continued to advance. In our haste to launch a defence, we had in fact only taken down six of these things. That was when I noticed, Seacroft was gone.

There were too many of them to deal with in such a confined space, so we changed tactics. Daniella blew apart the creatures nearest where we had come from, and I mopped up the rest, carving a path for us back towards the exit. One grabbed for my foot, but I kicked it in the jaw and sent it sprawling back into the cavern below.

My legs burned, and I stumbled against the walls grazing my face on the rock as I tried to run in the dark and reload my pistols. Ahead of me, Daniella kicked open the door and the light momentarily blinded me, before I launched out into the open air. It was a quick relief from the stagnant and metallic tainted air in the

The Graveyard Shift

caverns. We ran across the street and huddled against the exterior of the bar building.

But they didn't follow us.

I could still hear them, but they did not come from the same direction we did. And then I felt Daniella tug on my shirt sleeve.

"Uh... Reg?"

I turned to see where she was now pointing to, and felt my shoulders sag.

"You gotta be shittin' me."

The Lorengar were now clambering out onto rooftops, walking out from behind building shells, and four were arriving on horseback.

We had ourselves a genuine showdown shoot out.

18

Despite the fact we were firing at otherworldly creatures, the whole atmosphere felt electric. I've never felt more alive than I did right then. One of the Lorengar tried a straight run towards us and there was a momentary glance between myself and Daniella as we both thought 'what the hell is he doing' before blasting him apart, his insides collapsing onto the dirt street. As it turned out, it wasn't just their mouths we were up against. Each of them had guns, and the ones on the rooftops began firing at us, forcing us down the side of the building for cover.

Daniella switched out the shotgun, for a rifle, and began loading the ammunition as I continued to fire from my six shooters. I managed to take down three of the beasts that were crouched on the porch of an unfinished building across the street, with one of them crashing backwards through a rare completed window pane. The sound of the glass crunching under his body as he fell gave me a shudder. I'd been hit over the head with a whiskey bottle, and it had left its mark.

We moved down the street, Daniella ducking out from cover just enough to fire off a shot, before retreating and allowing me to follow up with quickfire rounds. Each time one of the Lorengar peeked out from behind cover, Daniella was there to blast them away. We must have gone through all twenty-five of those in the cave by now, and yet they kept coming. The bag of bullets on my shoulder was growing lighter by the minute, and although I did have my own shotgun still in the back holster, my accuracy with it was unknown.

As we finally reached the end of Main Street, one of the creatures launched off a low rooftop, and tackled Daniella to the ground. I moved towards her, a second charged me from behind a wagon stationed to my left. I unloaded the remaining bullets from my pistols, but as soon as this creature was down, another appeared from seemingly nowhere, running toward me at speed. I fumbled for more bullets, all the while conscious of Daniella rolling around on the floor trying to push the Lorengar away from her. I grasped the casings I needed but the creature running toward me roared and I dropped the bullets to the ground. I felt fire rising in my core, and I took a slow deep breath, reached round to my back and unleashed the shotgun.

"Fuck this."

I pumped the gun, and unloaded the first shot directly into the eye socket of the creature that had sprinted toward me. I moved along slowly and methodically, moving my shotgun to the left and blasting one of them from a high rooftop, his body falling like a sack of shit onto the ground where it appeared to explode upon impact. I was so distracted by my newfound concentration and accuracy with this booming weapon, I forgot about Daniella for a moment. Her scream pierced the air, audible over every shot I made, as the creature on top of her opened up its mouth and clamped it onto her shoulder. My practice with blades was much more longstanding, and so I reached into my belt, pulled out a small knife, and flicked it through the air. It made a whistling sound as it did so, and then a thwack as it embedded itself in the side of its head. I was relieved to see Daniella able to use her good shoulder to push it off her. Her dark blue shirt was now sodden with her blood, and her shoulder hang limply by her side. I was about to turn and head back toward her when I saw her grit her teeth, lean down and collect her shotgun, pump it single handedly, and march forward, her hair now dirty and matted against her face.

I couldn't help but smile as I saw this unstoppable force moving forward with deadly accuracy despite her injuries.

BOOM! She blew the head from the shoulders of the first to move toward her. BOOM! Another one bites the dust. The accuracy and speed she was able to empty the hot spent shells onto the ground, and reload with one hand left me in so much awe that I almost missed my own attackers moving toward me. Together, me and

Daniella marched forward taking down Lorengar left right and centre, until no more came for us.

We stood there surrounded by the bodies of demonic creatures that until a day prior we had no comprehension that they existed. All in all, there were over fifty of the creatures now slumped in heaps around this new town and its half finished buildings. Daniella sank to her knees and dropped her shotgun, and I rushed over to catch her from falling over completely.

"Miss Daniella, come on stay with me now."

She smiled up at me, and rolled her eyes.

"Like a demonic hickey is gonna take me out," she joked.

I took off my scarf, and attempted to tie it under her arm and tight across her shoulder to help stem the bleeding. It did seem to help, but it wouldn't hold for long.

"You have no idea what you've done."

The voice was not far away, but it was recognisable. Standing thirty feet away in the open was Samuel Seacroft. Daniella tried to get back up, but I held her down and motioned for her to stay there. In truth, her adrenaline had now worn off and she would only get herself killed. I gave her a brief tap on the shoulder, and then stood upright, making sure my shotgun was loaded, and I pumped it for good measure.

"We've blown your bitch ass to smithereens is what we've done. And you're next Seacroft."

The bravado in my voice was almost certainly betrayed by my eyes. In truth, my own adrenaline was

The Graveyard Shift

fading fast, and I was terrified. Seacroft seemed to recognise this, and began moving forward, but at a reserved pace.

"This place was going to save my people. We have been forced underground for centuries. This was all that was left of us, and you destroyed them all."

There was definitely a moment in my mind where I said 'oh shit' to myself. He was telling me to my face that I had just helped annihilate his entire species, or family or whatever the fuck they were. It was time to act. I raised the shotgun and pointed it directly at Seacroft's face. He stopped in his tracks.

"Go to hell."

I spoke with conviction and pulled the trigger.

Nothing happened.

I pulled it again.

Still nothing.

I opened the barrel and saw I had loaded two empty shells into the gun by mistake. That was all the excuse Seacroft needed. He launched towards me, and as he leapt into the air, his mouth unfolded and the teeth began rotating with fury. He smashed into me with such force, I felt a rib crack for sure, and the wind left me. It took everything I had to keep his mouth from latching down onto my flesh and doing much worse than hurt a shoulder. His eyes were now glowing a fierce red and all the strength I had was not going to be enough. My vision began to blur, and I could feel sweat building up on my brow.

BOOM!

An almighty explosion rocked one of the building frames beside us, and both me and Seacroft were launched sideways through the wooden wall of another building. My ears were ringing, and my skin had been peppered with wood splinters and dirt. I came to enough to notice the building we had been thrown through only had one main wall completed, and the entire structure was now beginning to fall. I managed to haul ass and jump free of the place before it cascaded down, collapsing completely. I scrambled back towards Daniella, but stopped when I saw what had caused the explosion. Daniella was sat where she had been the whole time, waving a stick of dynamite at me, smiling. Then I saw the crater. She had thrown a stick at the entrance to the nearest structure and it had blown not only the building apart, but also left a huge hole in the ground. I noticed deep in the crater, something was sparkling in the sunlight. It looked like some kind of crystal or mineral. I didn't know much about this sort of thing, but it was maybe a vein of quartz?

I didn't have long to contemplate that thought, as I heard the pieces of building being tossed aside by a now incredibly angry Samuel Seacroft, breaking free of the wreckage. I now had no weapon, Daniella and her dynamite were too far away, and there was definitely something else broken, as pain shot up my left arm, and my right knee. I noticed a brief glint in the dirt ahead and to my left. It was one of my larger blades. It must have fallen free when I was thrown through the air. But I'd never make it. Seacroft once again charged forward, his own blood now splattered across his formerly white suit from the wounds on his face. I closed my eyes and accepted my fate.

And then nothing.

I opened my eyes to an astonishing sight. Samuel Seacroft was banging against some kind of white translucent wall. I could hear him roaring, but it was almost muffled.

"I cannot hold him for long."

The sweet familiar voice to my right was a welcome one. Penny was stood directly over the vein of minerals, her hands thrust in front of her. She was somehow generating this with one of her incantations. It was becoming harder for her to do so, and I could not help but notice her feet began to disappear.

"Penny, your legs," was all I could muster.

"Yes! I'm using my energy to keep him back. You only have a minute! Hurry!"

I didn't have time to contemplate what she was saying to me, I simply turned and dived for the knife, gripping it by the handle. I looked back and all that remained of Penny's image was her arms and her head. But then I saw more familiar images appear, and the smile spread across my face once more. Ralph and Jean both now stood over the same vein Penny did, and they spoke to each other, but I couldn't hear what they said. It looked like they were trying to memorise something. Then suddenly, Penny evaporated into nothingness, the barrier fell and Seacroft continued to charge towards me.

Then two burst of light struck him in each shoulder, knocking him to his knees. I snapped my head round, and saw Jean and Ralph concentrating hard. As they fired another two blasts of energy at Seacroft, they too vanished from sight. I hoped I would see them again, but this did seem to have a degree of finality to it. I didn't waste it.

I turned to face Seacroft just as he veered up to launch at me again, and as he threw his head forwards, I thrust the entirety of the blade and half of my arm into his open razor sharp mouth with such force that it burst through the back of his skull. His entire body went limp on my arm, and without the strength to hold him up, we both collapsed into a heap.

I let my breath escape me, and turned back toward where I had seen the ghosts of my friends, the inhabitants of the graveyard shift. But they were gone. I closed my eyes, and fell into a comforting sleep.

EPILOGUE

"Stay still Reg!"

I jerked my arm away from Daniella as the pain seared through my skin. This was the third time I'd gotten a monumental sized splinter wedged in my hand this week. It felt like the whole damn town was trying to slowly bleed me dry. In the two months since we killed Seacroft and his other minions, several things had been discovered and come into the light.

It became known that Samuel Seacroft was a murderer and he was credited with the deaths of over fifty people. That of course was just the ones in this lifetime. There was no telling how many he had killed over the centuries. He was also stripped of the land in San Francisco, and it was handed over to the city to maintain. But the biggest surprise of all, was that the land being used to build Wealdstone actually belonged to my grandfather. As it turned out, Seacroft had lured me to San Francisco in the first place to kill me. I was the last living heir to the land that he had already started building on. I'd had no idea that Grandpa had bought the land cheaply when he was thinking about building a home by the sea. When the authorities found out, the titles were transferred to me.

I had no money to speak of, and no way to continue the construction of the place, and so I invited the kind people of Crossroads to help me, with the promise of a home for each and every one of them who helped, free of charge. Things are moving slowly, but there are already nearly a hundred of us living here now. I did what I believed my Grandpa was planning. I built my little cabin overlooking the sea on top of a nearby cliff. And then, I started the Wealdstone Cemetery. I figured we would need a place to lay our friends and family to rest once the town was completed, and I've always been a grave digger. Even though there were only four graves in this new plot, those of people who had asked if they could be buried overlooking the ocean, I still spend time at night patrolling and contemplating what had happened to us all. I never did see the spirits of Penny, Ralph or Jean again. It seemed as though they had indeed used up their very existence to help save me and this place, and I will never forget it.

I do have new companions on the graveyard shift though. Since some of the mineral veins were unearthed during the construction of some of our new buildings, I noticed each night one or two new spirits wandering around. I don't mind them, they just want someone to talk to. And from what some of them tell me, there's no

The Graveyard Shift

actual Heaven or Hell for them to drift off to, so they may as well keep me company.

"Yeah well you try having a bunch of four-foot splinters of wood sticking out of your palm and see how you like it!"

Daniella threw the slither of wood in the trash, and dabbed at the trickle of blood that appeared.

"Man up Reg, it's better than a thousand needle sharp teeth chomping on your flesh."

She did have a point.

Daniella decided to stick around. In her time, this place had been her home. She showed me where her house would be built before long, but I reminded her that the particular plot of land was not part of my boundary and was already earmarked by the Miles family for a family home. She didn't argue with me, just gave me that wry smile she has become famous around here for.

"I know. I'm just saying, eventually, it'll be mine."

Daniella has been of great comfort to me, and I did offer her the chance to build her own home in Wealdstone, but she declined and every night she goes back to the Silverton Ranch, alone. She says it's her penance for failing not one but two versions of the same woman. I haven't asked for details, as I still don't like to pry into her past.

Besides, I have a quest of my own to undertake. I've grown into somewhat of a protector lately, and there were even calls for me to take over as Sheriff when the current one decided to step down. As it turns out, mopping up body parts in a brothel can really put you off the job. But I have loftier goals in mind. From what Daniella tells me, Wealdstone will become front and centre for many supernatural wars to come in the years ahead. I cannot afford to let this place fall without a protector. And after the things I have seen, I know there must be a way of prolonging my existence.

I will not abandon Wealdstone.

And death will not stop me.

REGINALD T. FOX
WILL RETURN

Printed in Great Britain
by Amazon